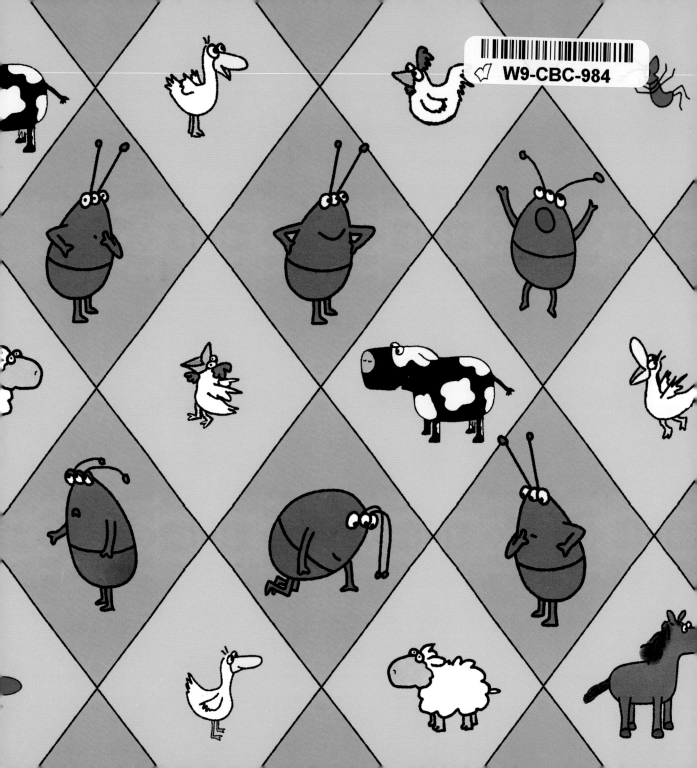

PJ Library, a program of the Harold Grinspoon Foundation
67 Hunt Street, Suite 100
Agawam, MA 01001
U.S.A.

Designed by Michael Grinley

First Edition
10 9 8 7 6 5 4 3 2 1
052125K1/B1651/A2
Printed in China

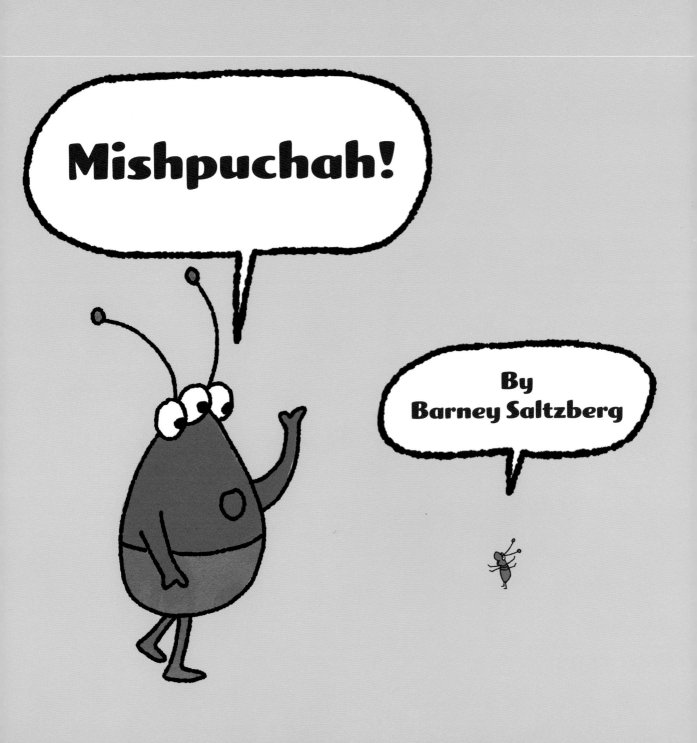

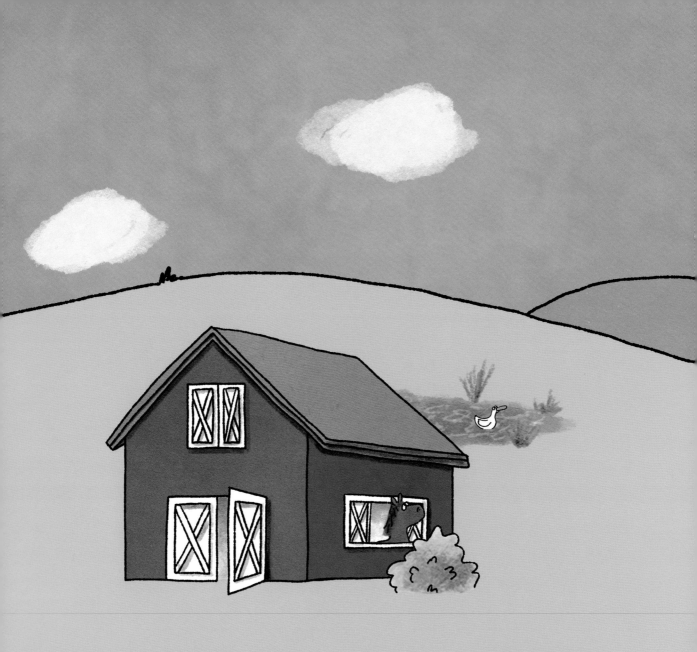

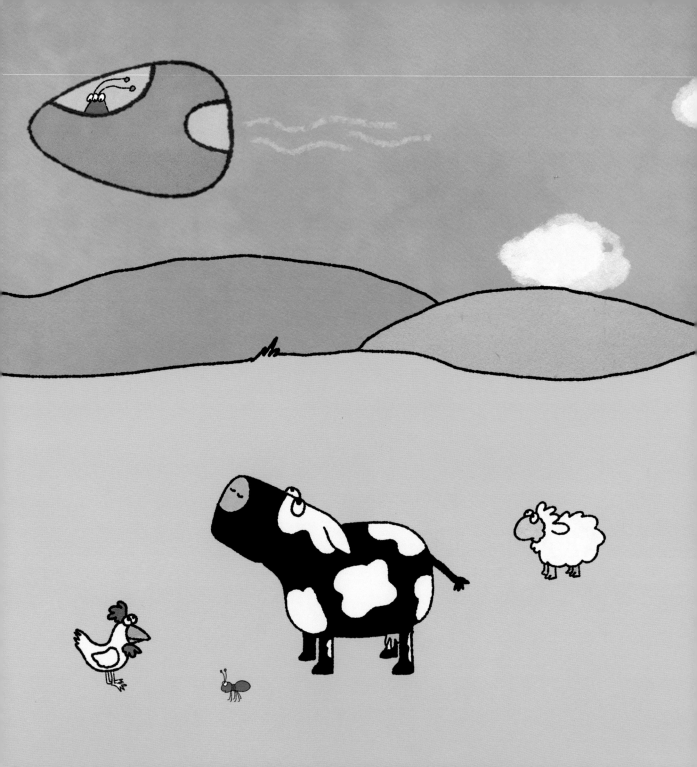

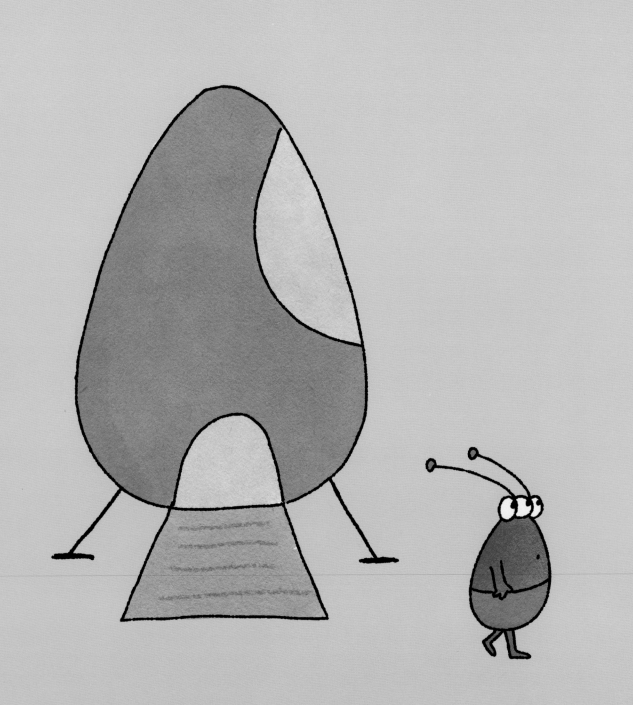

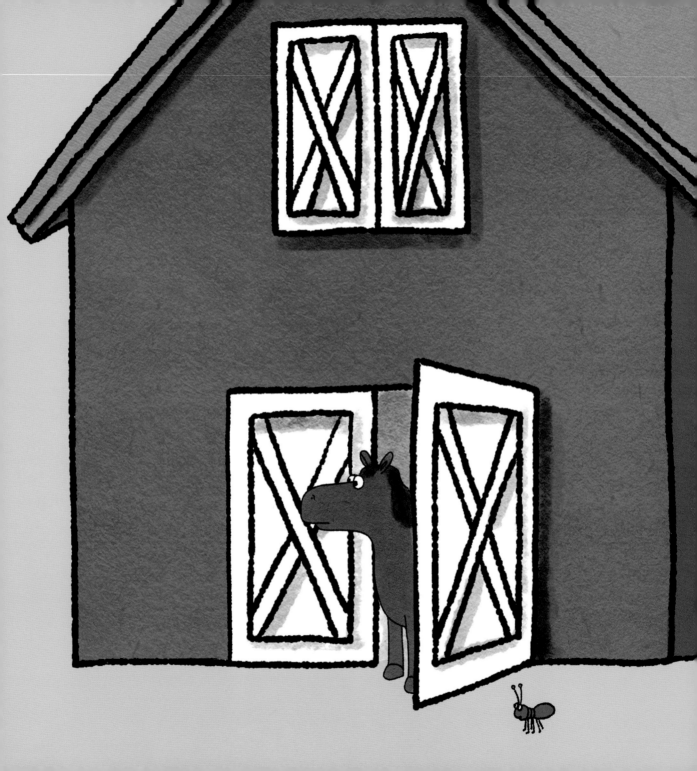

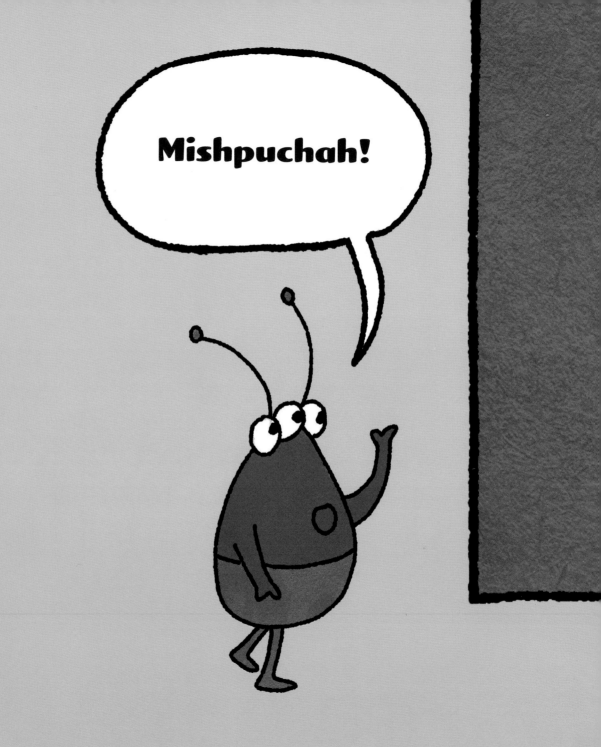

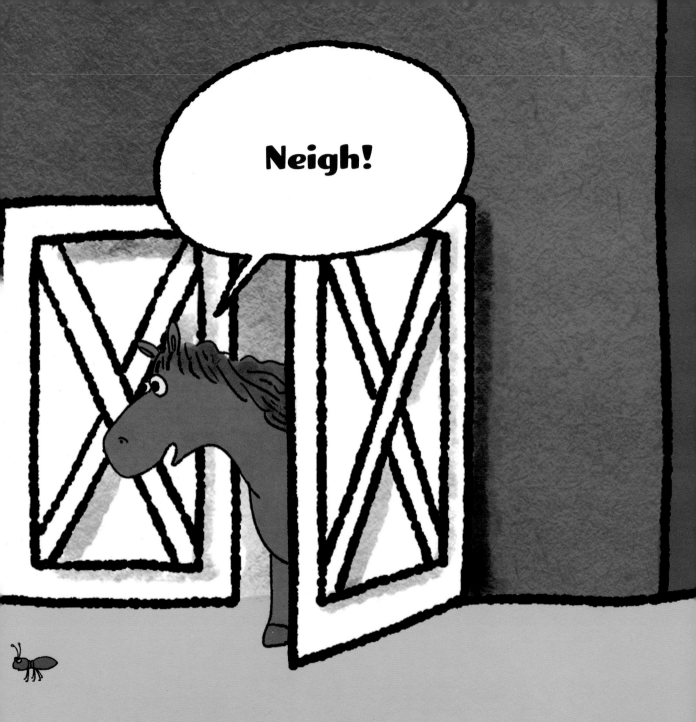

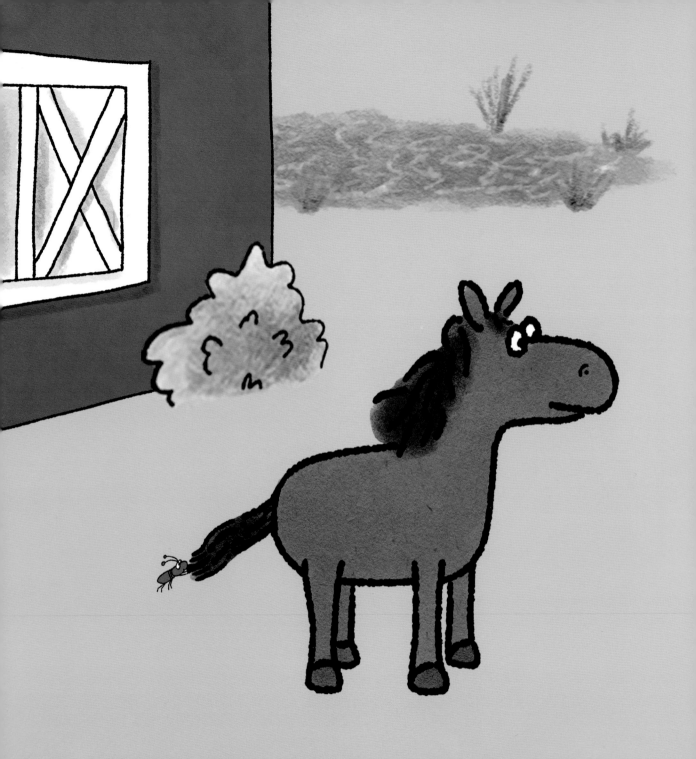

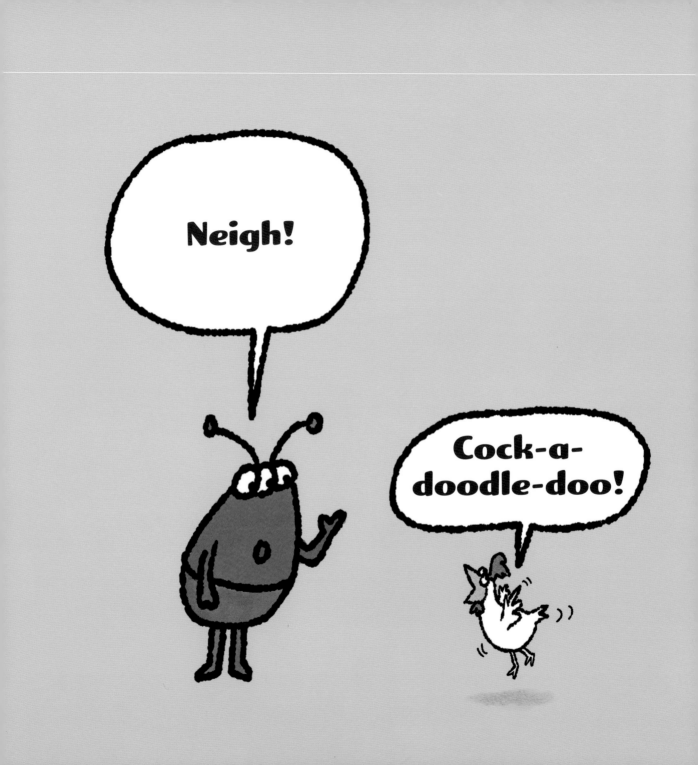

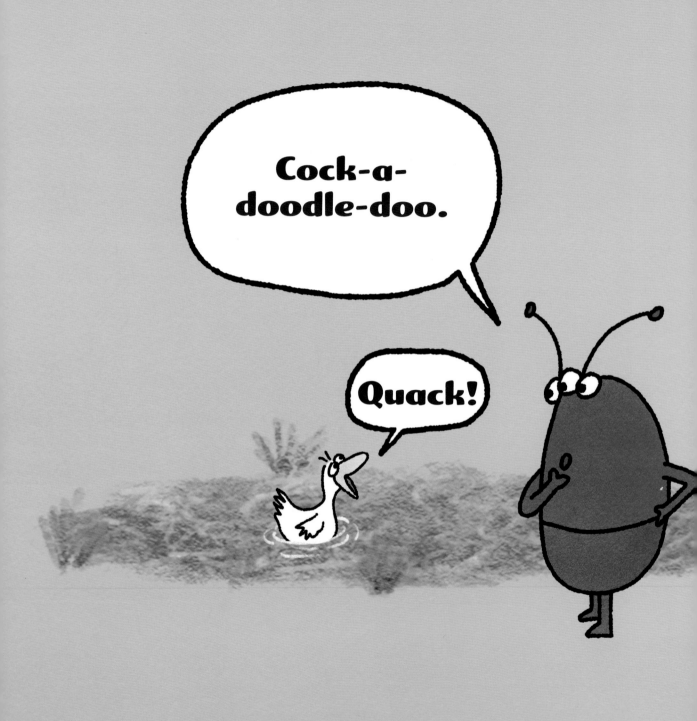

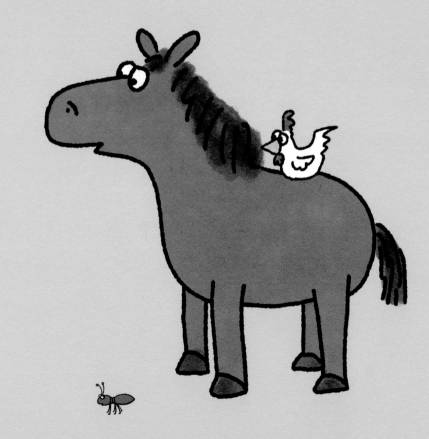

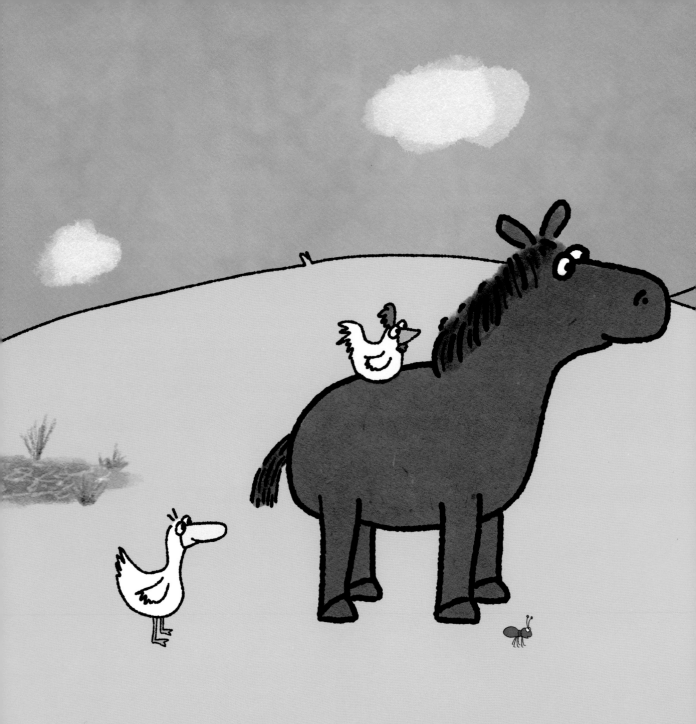

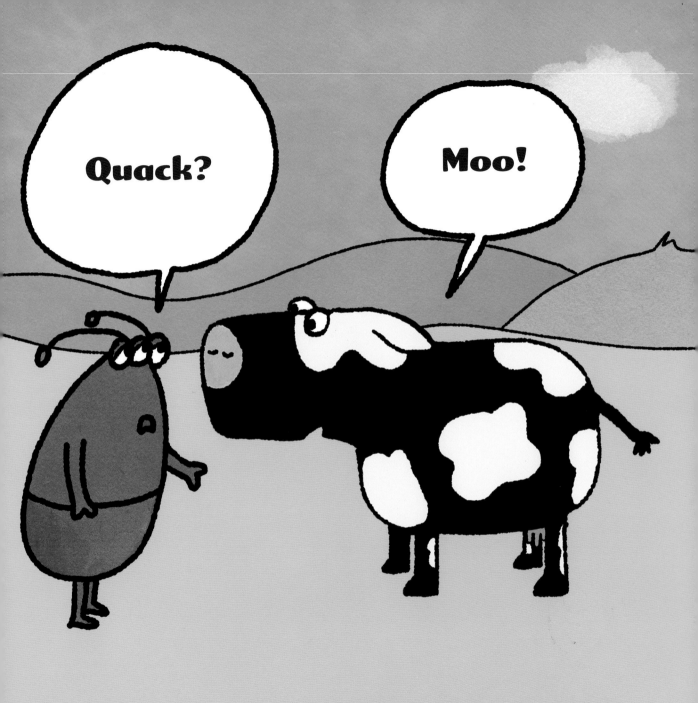

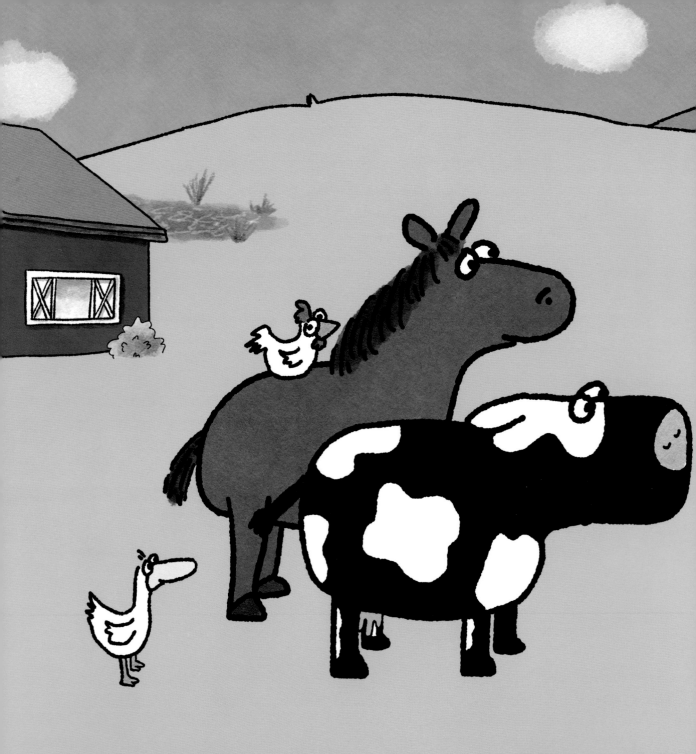

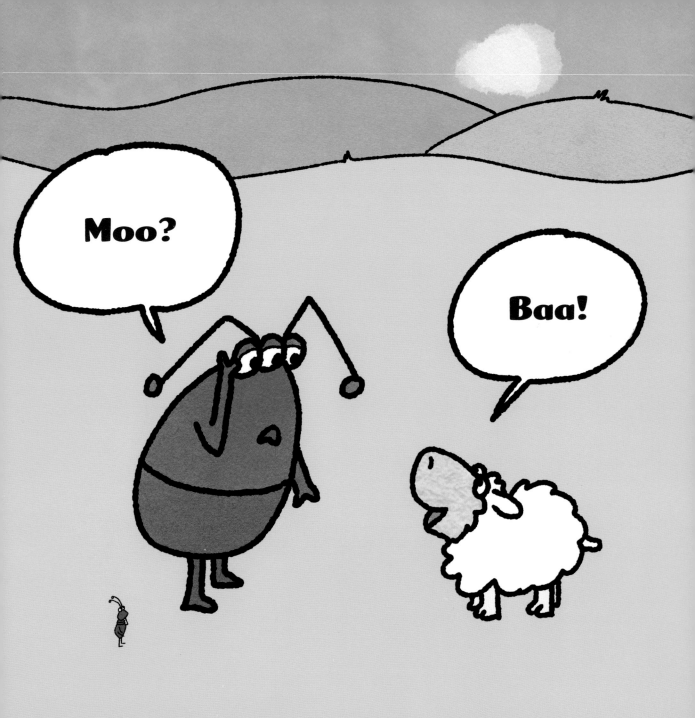

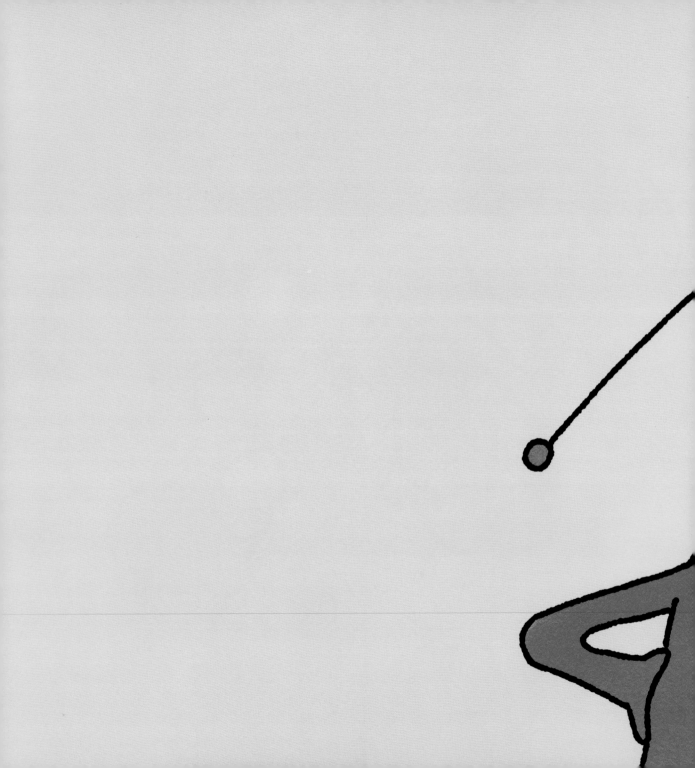

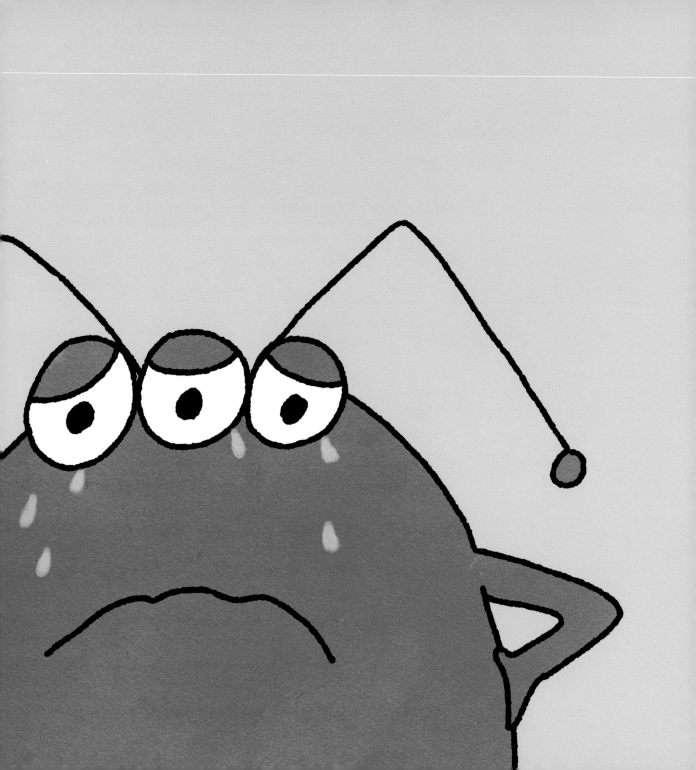

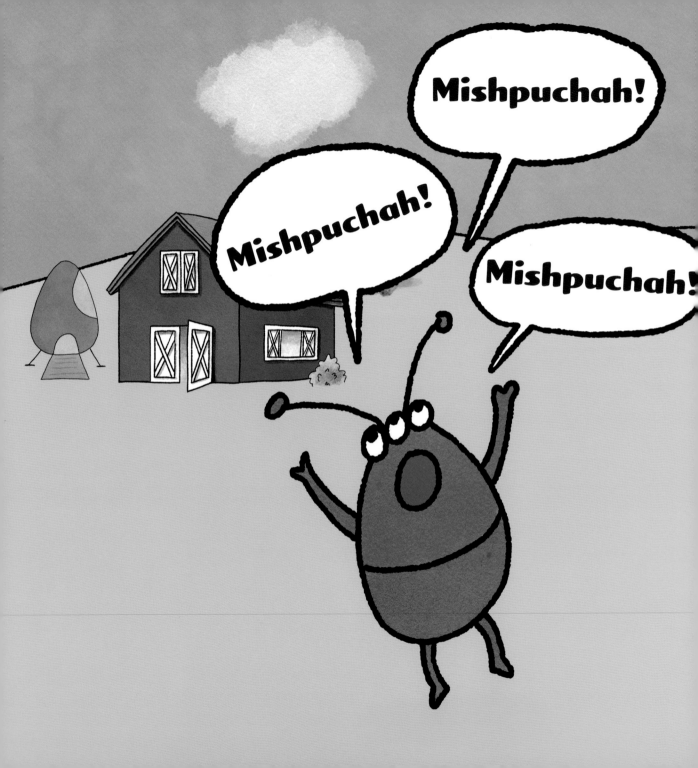

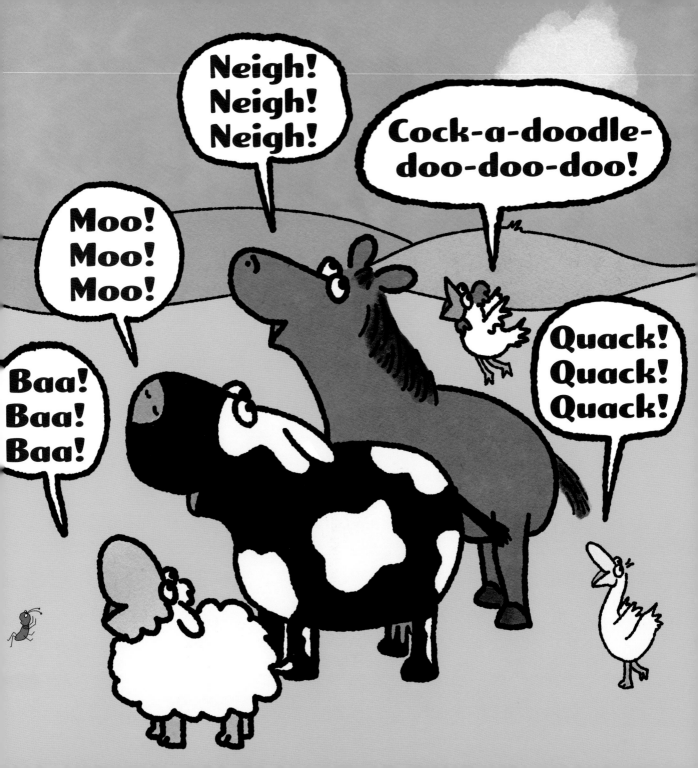

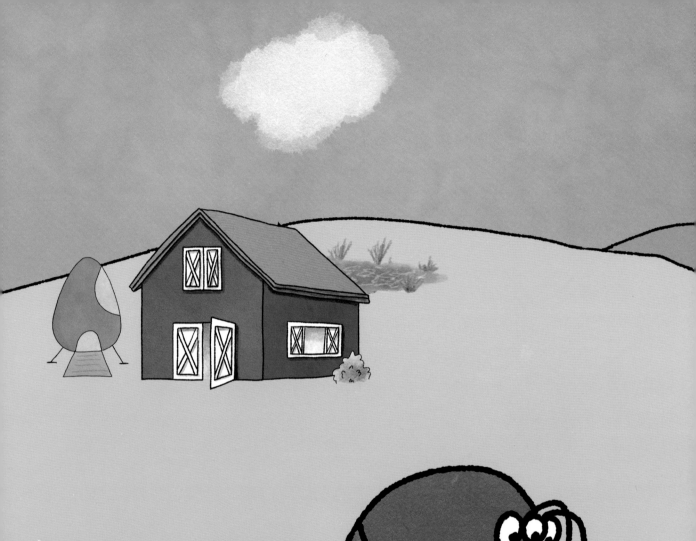

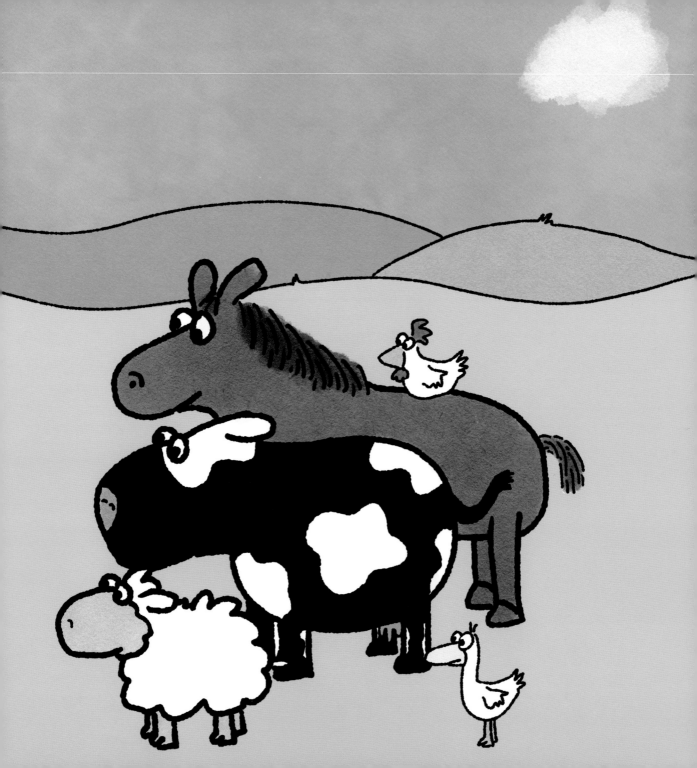

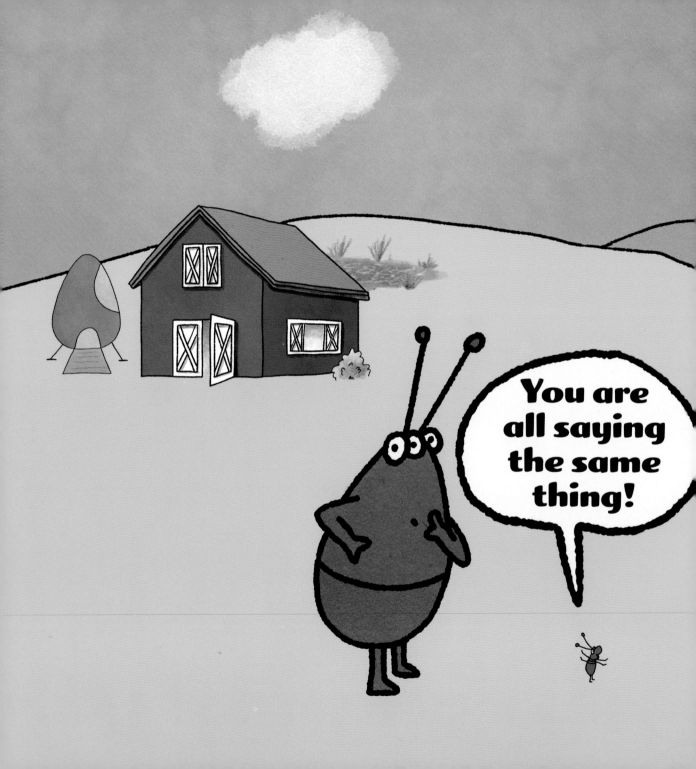

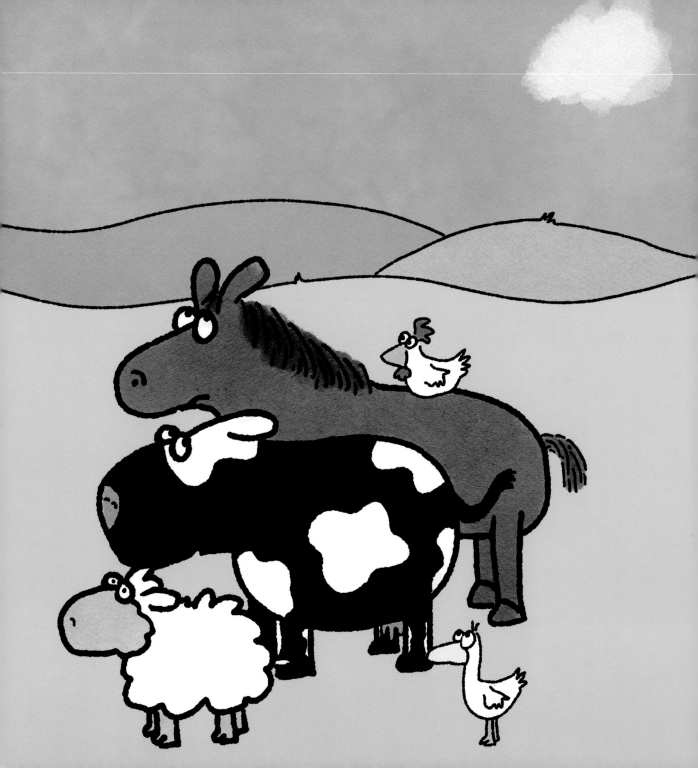

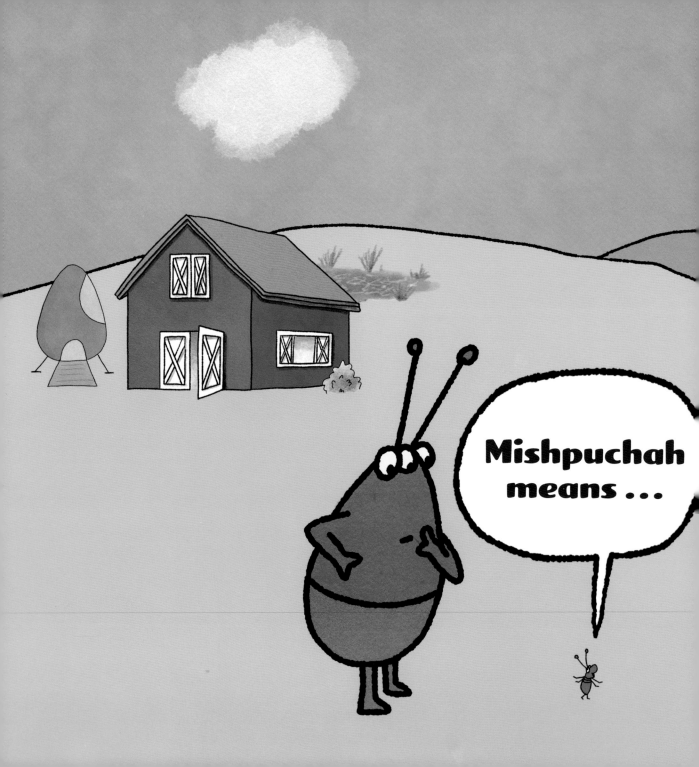

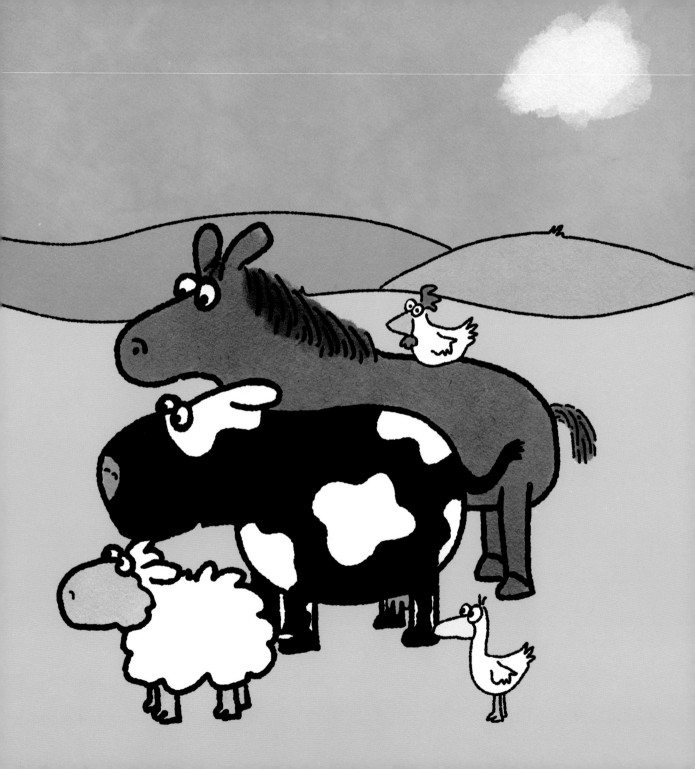

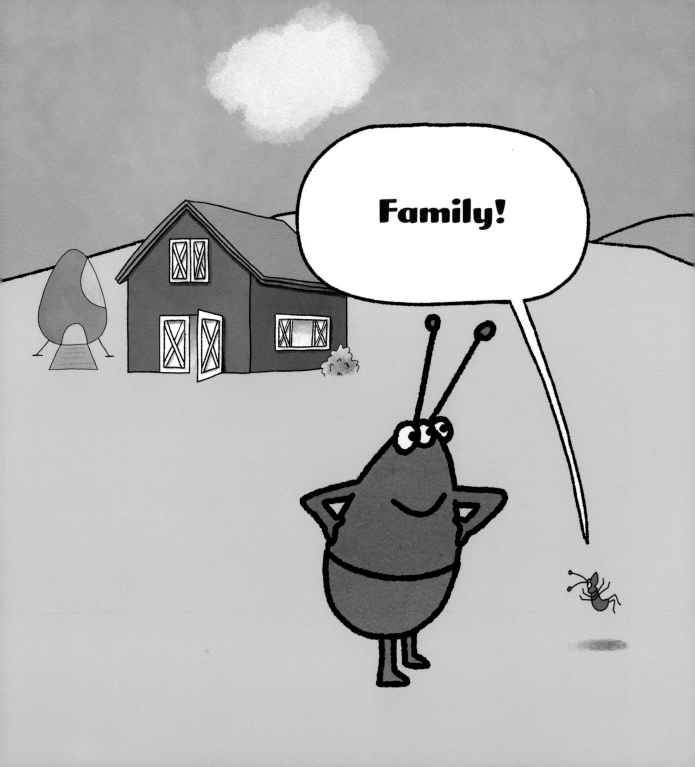

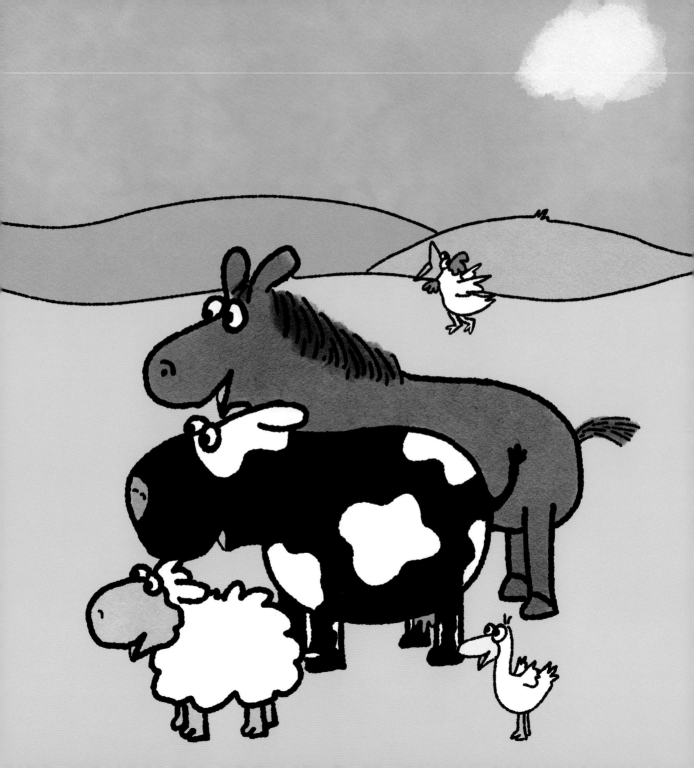

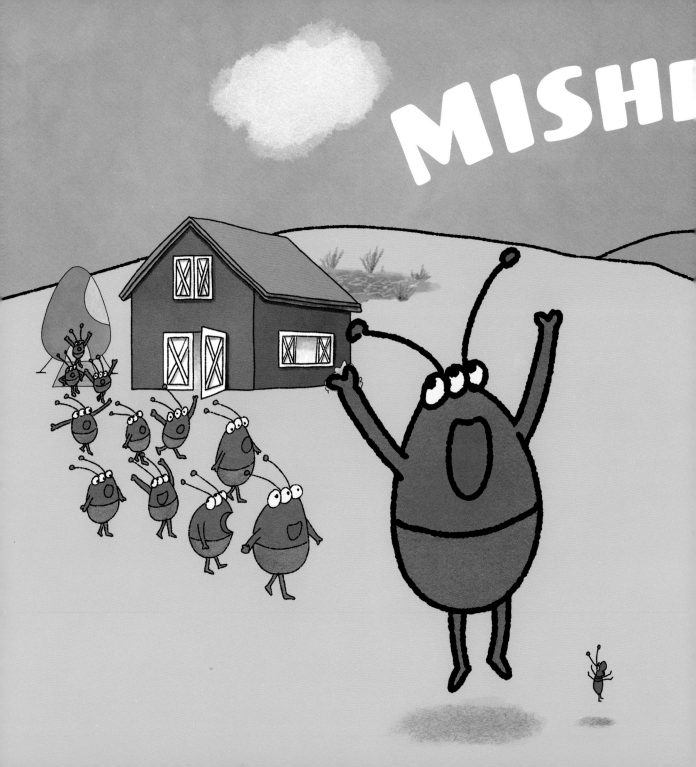

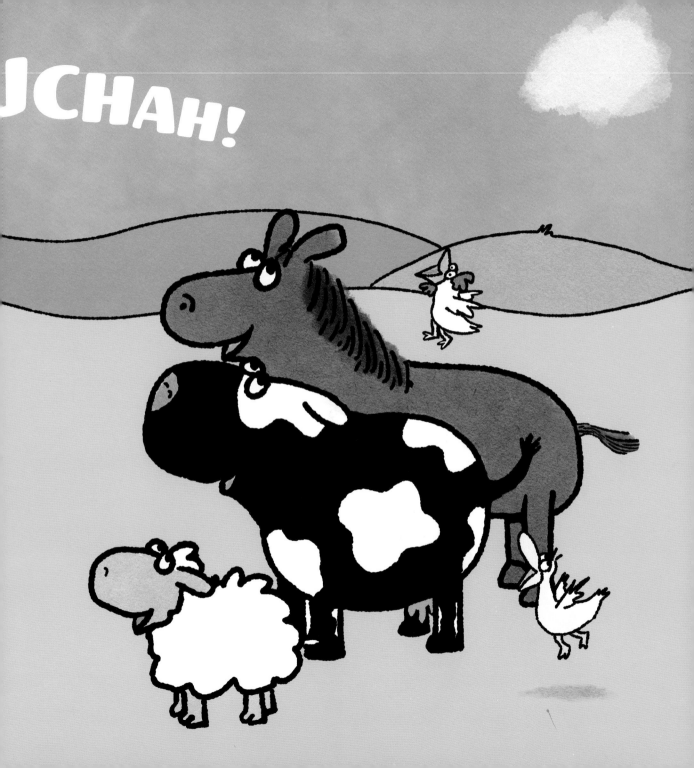

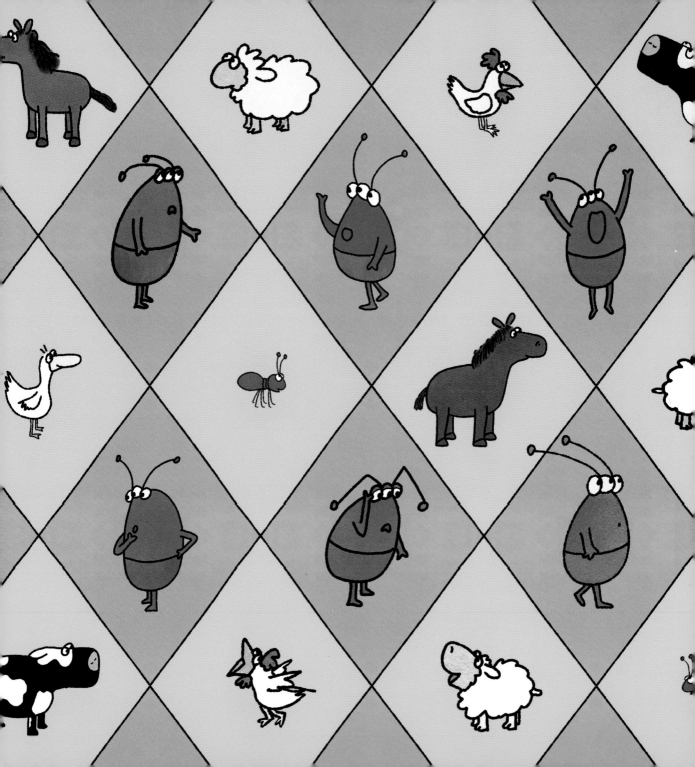